Molly the Great's Messy Bed:

A Book About Responsibility

by Shelley Marshall   Illustrated by Ben Mahan

Molly the Great does not want to make her bed. But she needs to do her part! That is what responsible superheroes do. How can she do a better job next time? **Let's read!**

Enslow Elementary
an imprint of
Enslow Publishers, Inc.
40 Industrial Road
Box 398
Berkeley Heights, NJ 07922
USA
http://www.enslow.com

"Mom!" Molly calls. "May I go to the zoo with Ben? May I? May I, please?"

Molly wants to see the elephants so much!

"Yes," says Mom, "after you make your bed."

"No!" Molly yells. "Superheroes do not make beds!"

Uh-oh. Molly gets sent to her room.

"You may come out when you are ready to make your bed," says Molly's mom.

Molly is not ready. She does not make her bed. She makes new clothes for Princess Polly, instead.

Molly has a great idea. Princess Polly will ride an elephant.
Molly has a toy elephant. Where can it be?

Wait a minute. Is she sitting on it? No!

Molly looks in the toy box. Her elephant is not there.

It is not in her closet.

Molly remembers where the elephant is. It is in her bed!

Wow! What a mess!

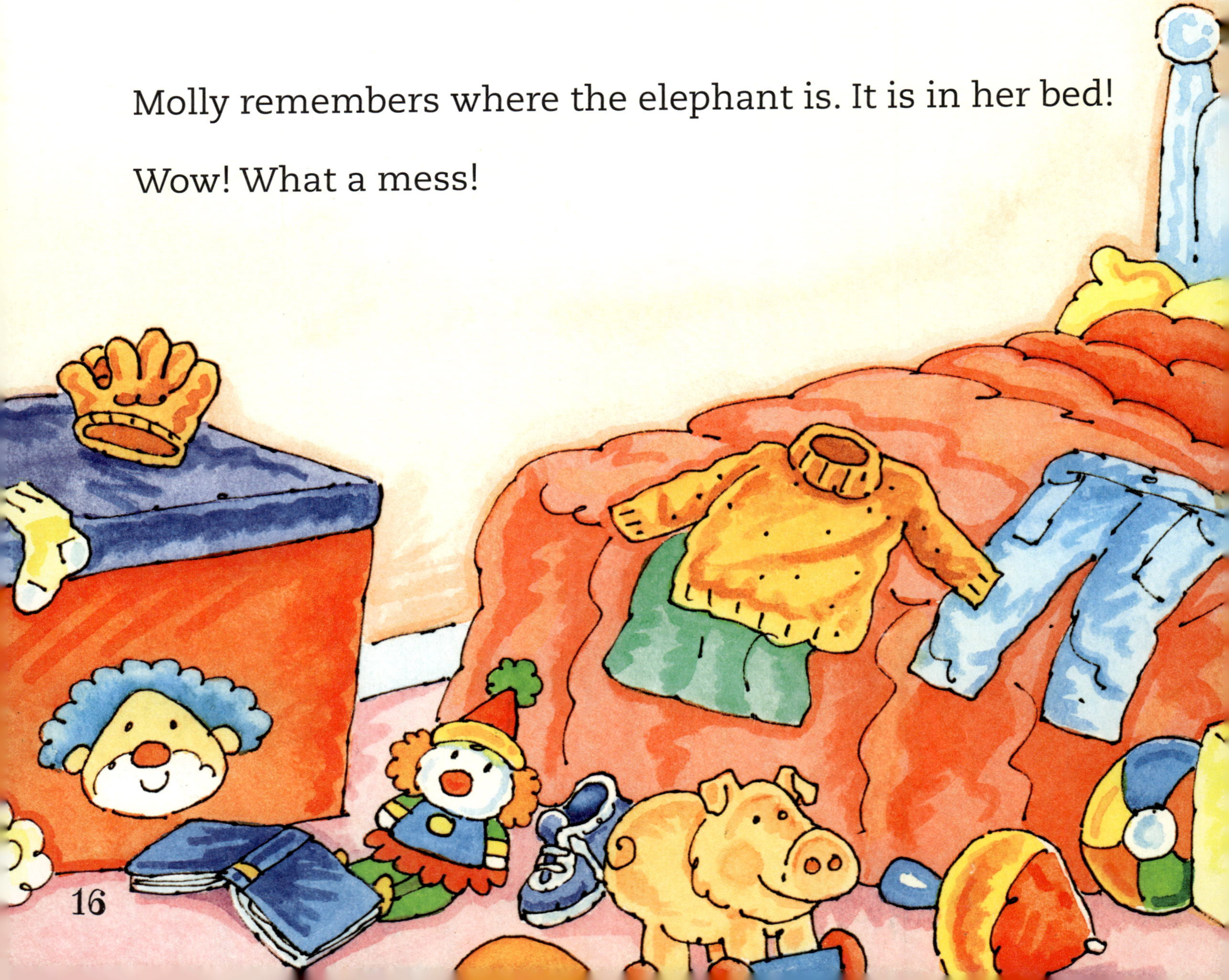

"I guess I had better make my bed," says Molly.
Molly picks up her toys, too.

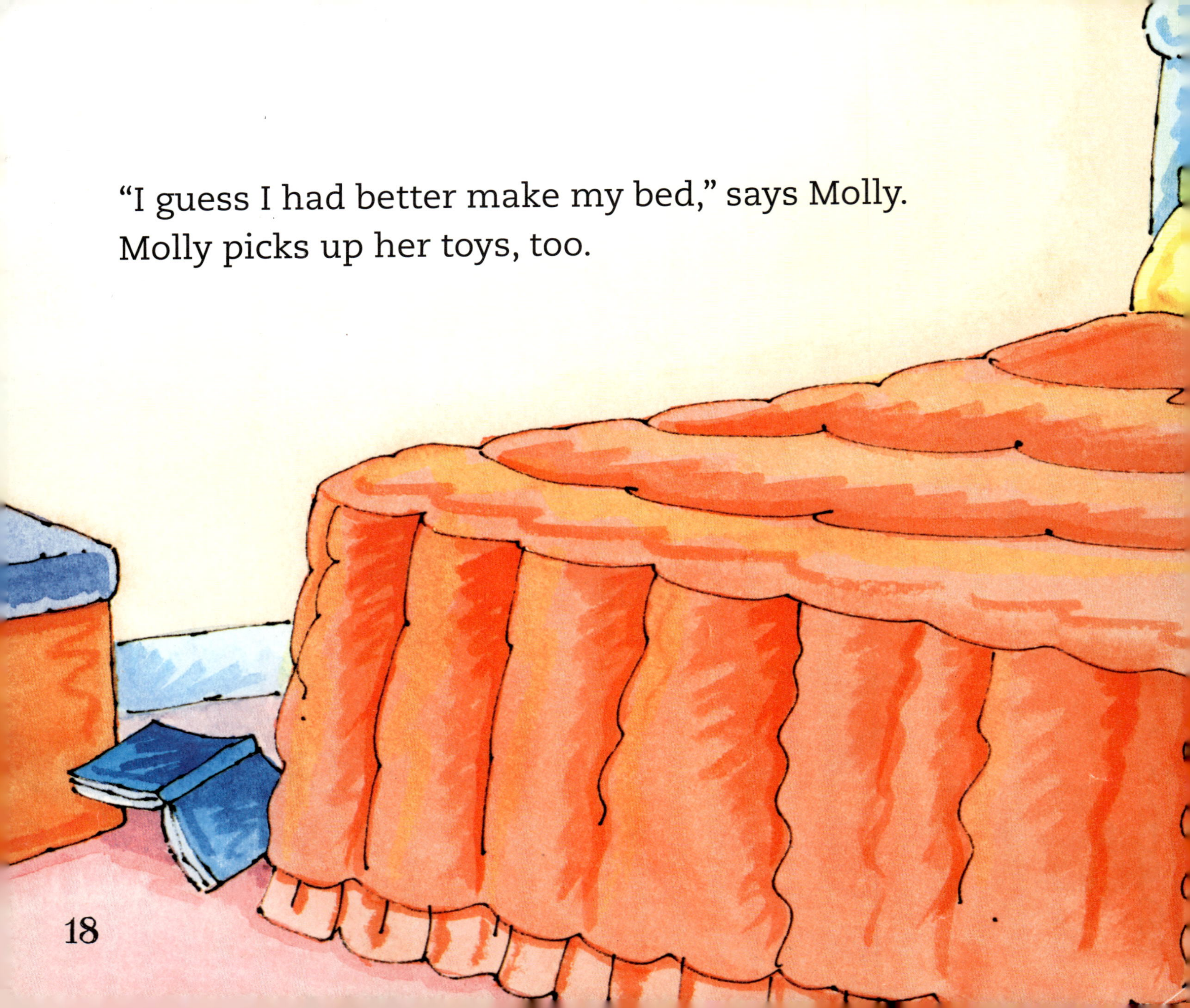

"Mom! Mom! Come see!" Molly calls.

Mom laughs. "Your room looks great!"

“We all have chores we have to do,” Mom says. “Thank you for doing your part. You are a super family member!”

Read More About Being Responsible

Books

Kroll, Virginia L. *Jason Takes Responsibility*. Morton Grove, IL: Albert Whitman & Company, 2005.

Loewen, Nancy. *Do I Have To? Kids Talk About Responsibility*. Minneapolis, MN: Picture Window Books, 2005.

Web Site

Kids Next Door
www.hud.gov/kids/people.html

Enslow Elementary, an imprint of Enslow Publishers, Inc.

Enslow Elementary® is a registered trademark of Enslow Publishers, Inc.

Library of Congress Cataloging-in-Publication Data
Marshall, Shelley.
Molly the Great's messy bed : a book about responsibility / by Shelley Marshall.
p. cm. — (Character education with Super Ben and Molly the Great)
ISBN 978-0-7660-3517-1
1. Responsibility—Juvenile literature. I. Title.
BJ1451.M35 2010
170—dc22
2009008305

ISBN-13: 978-0-7660-3742-7 (paperback edition)

Printed in the United States of America

112009 Lake Book Manufacturing, Inc., Melrose Park, IL

10 9 8 7 6 5 4 3 2 1

To Our Readers: We have done our best to make sure all Internet Addresses in this book were active and appropriate when we went to press. However, the author and the publisher have no control and assume no liability for the material available on those Internet sites or on other Web sites they may link to. Any comments or suggestions can be sent by e-mail to comments@enslow.com or to the address on the back cover.

Enslow Publishers, Inc. is committed to printing our books on recycled paper. The paper in every book contains 10% to 30% post-consumer waste (PCW). The cover board on the outside of every book contains 100% PCW. Our goal is to do our part to help young people and the environment too!